There Was an Odd Princess Who Swallowed a Pea

Crunch!

by Jennifer Ward

illustrated by Lee Calderon

Marshall Cavendish Children

All rights reserved
Marshall Cavendish Corporation
99 White Plains Road, Tarrytown, NY 10591
www.marshallcavendish.us/kids

Library of Congress Cataloging-in-Publication Data
Ward, Jennifer.
There was an odd princess who swallowed a pea / by Jennifer Ward ;
illustrated by Lee Calderon. — 1st ed.
p. cm.
Summary: Set in a castle, this variation on the traditional, cumulative
rhyme looks at the consequences of a princess's strange diet.
ISBN 978-0-7614-5822-7 (hardcover) — ISBN 978-0-7614-6065-7 (ebook)
1. Folk songs, English—England—Texts. [1. Folk songs. 2. Nonsense
verses.] I. Calderon, Lee, 1962– ill. II. Little old lady who swallowed a
fly. III. Title.
PZ8.3.W2135Thj 2011   782.42—dc22   [E]   2010044478

The illustrations are rendered in digital media.
Book design by Vera Soki
Editor: Marilyn Brigham

Printed in China (E)
First edition
10 9 8 7 6 5 4 3 2 1

mc Marshall Cavendish
Children

To my own little princess, Kelly
—J.W.

To my mom; my wife, Yvette; and my daughter, Sophia . . .
once a princess, always a princess
—L.C.

There was an odd princess . . .

. . . who swallowed a pea.
Sipped her tea with that tiny pea.
Then burped with glee.

There was an odd princess who swallowed a slipper.
It made her feel chipper to eat that glass slipper.

She swallowed the slipper right after the pea.
Then burped with glee.

There was an odd princess who swallowed a **crown**.
She munched it down, that sparkling crown.
She swallowed the crown right after the slipper.
She swallowed the slipper right after the pea.
Then burped with glee.

There was an odd princess who swallowed a **rose**.
It tickled her nose, that red-petaled rose.
She swallowed the rose right after the crown.
She swallowed the crown right after the slipper.
She swallowed the slipper right after the pea.
Then burped with glee.

There was an odd princess who swallowed a **wand**.
She nibbled that wand by the castle pond.
She swallowed the wand right after the rose.
She swallowed the rose right after the crown.
She swallowed the crown right after the slipper.
She swallowed the slipper right after the pea.
Then burped with glee.

There was an odd princess . . .

. . . who swallowed a **witch**.

Without a hitch, she gobbled that witch.

She swallowed the witch right after the wand.

She swallowed the wand right after the rose.

She swallowed the rose right after the crown.

She swallowed the crown right after the slipper.

She swallowed the slipper right after the pea.

Then burped with glee.

There was an odd princess who swallowed a **prince**.
Without a wince, she swallowed that prince.
She swallowed the prince right after the witch.
She swallowed the witch right after the wand.
She swallowed the wand right after the rose.
She swallowed the rose right after the crown.
She swallowed the crown right after the slipper.
She swallowed the slipper right after the pea.
Then burped with glee.

There was an odd princess who swallowed a **queen**.
Isn't that mean? She swallowed a queen!
She swallowed the queen right after the prince.
She swallowed the prince right after the witch.
She swallowed the witch right after the wand.
She swallowed the wand right after the rose.
She swallowed the rose right after the crown.
She swallowed the crown right after the slipper.
She swallowed the slipper right after the pea.
Then burped with glee.

There was an odd princess . . .

. . . who swallowed a   .
Slurped it down her delicate throat.

She swallowed the moat right after the queen.
She swallowed the queen right after the prince.
She swallowed the prince right after the witch.
She swallowed the witch right after the wand.
She swallowed the wand right after the rose.
She swallowed the rose right after the crown.
She swallowed the crown right after the slipper.
She swallowed the slipper right after the pea.
Then burped with glee.

There was an odd princess who swallowed a **castle**.
Without a hassle, she gulped that castle.
She swallowed the castle right after the moat.
She swallowed the moat right after the queen.
She swallowed the queen right after the prince.
She swallowed the prince right after the witch.
She swallowed the witch right after the wand.
She swallowed the wand right after the rose.
She swallowed the rose right after the crown.
She swallowed the crown right after the slipper.
She swallowed the slipper right after the pea.
Then burped with glee.

There was an odd princess
who burst with laughter.

And can you guess . . .

. . . she lived happily ever after.